Uncle Arthur's
BEDTIME STORIES
Twenty - Ninth Series

Story hour with Daddy is always a happy time.

Uncle Arthur's

Bedtime Stories

Twenty-Ninth Series

By ARTHUR S. MAXWELL

Price: 3/-

Registered at Stationers' Hall by

THE STANBOROUGH PRESS LTD.,

WATFORD, HERTS., ENGLAND

—CONTENTS—

Copyright, 1952
THE STANBOROUGH PRESS LTD.,
Watford, Herts., England

—PREFACE—

WHEN you read "Twenty-ninth Series" on this little book you may wonder what it means. Only this: that these stories have been coming out every year since 1924, with never a break, through peace and war, through good times and bad, and this is number twenty-nine.

All the years I have been writing these stories I have tried to make sure that every one is based on fact and that every one teaches some character-building lesson. The same principles have been followed in preparing the stories in this latest series. I hope you will enjoy them. I think you will.

Often people say to me, Where do you get all these stories, every one different from all the hundreds of others in the previous series? The answer is that they come to me from all over the world. Sometimes a little boy will tell me one. Sometimes a little girl will write me pages and pages of rigmarole with a lovely story tucked away somewhere in it all. And, of course, parents write to me, too. You may write as well, if you wish. If you know of some special experience that might make a *Bedtime Story*, I shall be delighted to hear from you. Address me in care of the Publishers and they'll send it on.

UNCLE ARTHUR.

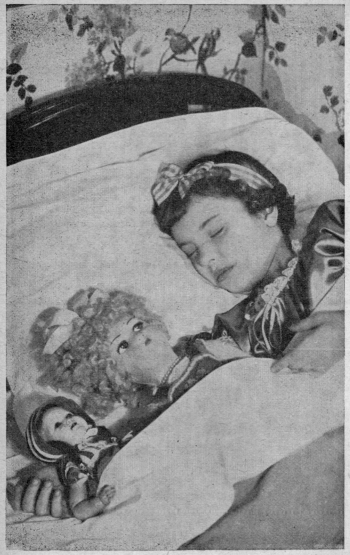

Though Priscilla was her favourite doll, Edith decided to give her to Laura.

They Gave Their Best

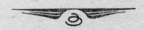

IT was just a week before Christmas and every-body was thinking about Christmas presents. Edith and Eva were making lists of things they hoped they would find in their stockings. Mamma watched them awhile and then said,

"You know, dears, you have such a lot of toys already, why don't you give some of them away to children who may not get many presents this year?"

Edith and Eva looked up in surprise. They hadn't thought about doing anything like that.

"Are there any children who won't get presents this Christmas?" asked Edith.

"Why, yes," said Mamma. "Lots of them. And some live very near us. You know about poor Laura and Katie who lost their Mamma and Daddy in the car accident. They must be feeling very sad and lonely."

"Of course!" said Edith, who always had a very tender heart. "They won't have anybody to give them presents this year—except the lady they are staying with. And I don't think she likes children very much."

"Let's look through our things," said Eva, "and see what we can find."

Mamma left them to talk it over. Soon they were turning out their toy cupboard, piling dolls, woolly animals, balls, building blocks, paints, crayons, and I don't know what else, on the kitchen floor.

"Oh, dear, which shall we give?" sighed Eva, sitting down in the middle of all the toys.

"I don't know," said Edith. "But I suppose we should choose something extra special for poor Laura and Katie."

"Yes," said Eva, sitting down beside her. "I suppose we should. Do you know what I am going to give?"

"No, what?" asked Edith.

"Black Beauty," said Eva.

"Oh, no, not your precious cuddly dog!" said Edith.

"Yes, I am," said Eva, decidedly.

"Then I shall give Priscilla," said Edith. "Laura will love her. I'm sure she will."

"That's the dolly you like most," said Eva.

"I know," said Edith, picking up Priscilla and giving her a big hug.

Just then Mamma came back into the kitchen.

"Oh, my dears!" she exclaimed. "What a mess! I mean, what a lot of toys! Have you

Ⓢ Studio Lisa
PICTURE OPPOSITE : *After making her generous gift, Eva enjoyed her Christmas dinner all the more.*

© Keystone

These delightful dolls are on their way to make some little girls happy.

made up your minds which you would like to give away?"

"Yes," said Edith. "Eva says she's going to give Black Beauty, and I'm going to give Priscilla."

"Oh, but, darlings, those are your very best toys!" said Mamma.

"That's right," said Eva. "That's what we want to give."

"But if you give them away you can't get them back," said Mamma.

"We know," said Edith.

"But Eva, you take Black Beauty to bed with you every night. Can you really spare him?"

"Uh-huh," grunted Eva.

"And Edith, you have always loved Priscilla so much. Are you sure you really want to give her away?"

"Uh-huh," grunted Edith, nodding her head.

"You little darlings!" cried Mamma, sitting down on the floor between them and putting her arms around them both. "I think you are the dearest, sweetest little girls in all the world."

Next day Edith gave Priscilla a wash and put on her very nicest dress. Then she helped Eva clean up Black Beauty and tie a new ribbon round his neck. After that they put the two lovely toys in a basket, covered them with a cloth, and waited, impatiently, for Christmas Eve.

At last the big day came. Mamma said the two children could go round to see Laura and

Katie by themselves, which they were very pleased to do.

Holding the basket between them, they knocked on the door.

"Merry Christmas!" they said, smiling, as the door opened, and they stepped inside.

"Merry Christmas!" said Laura and Katie. "But what have you got in that basket?"

"Guess!" cried Edith.

"Guess!" cried Eva.

"We couldn't guess," said Laura and Katie together.

Then Edith and Eva set the basket on the floor and pulled off the cover.

"Oh!" cried Laura and Katie. "How lovely!"

"And this is for you," said Edith, holding up Priscilla to Laura.

"And this is for you," said Eva, handing Black Beauty to Katie.

"Oh, thank you, thank you!" cried the two little girls together as they danced and jumped about for joy.

"You'll never guess," said Laura presently, as she stroked Priscilla's lovely golden hair, "but this is the very thing I asked Jesus to send me for Christmas."

When Edith and Eva got home Mamma was waiting for them.

"Why, I never saw you two so happy before!" she said.

"Oh, Mamma!" they cried. "You should have

seen how happy we made those two little girls!"

"That's the real Christmas spirit," said Mamma. "Sharing happiness we make ourselves happier."

"But do you know what one of the girls said?" said Edith.

"No," said Mamma. "What did she say?"

"She said she had been asking Jesus to send her a doll for Christmas just like my Priscilla."

"How wonderful!" said Mamma.

"Yes," said Edith. "How glad I am I gave my best!"

"So am I," said Eva.

"And so am I," said Mamma, giving them both a great big kiss.

© Keystone

Steeplejacks at work on top of the world's tallest building.

Steve the Steeplejack

LITTLE Steve had often seen his daddy climb up high and dangerous places, like church steeples and tall chimneys, and someday, he told himself, he would be a steeplejack, too.

It happened much sooner than he dreamed.

One day, as he was walking into town, he saw a little group of people standing outside the old Methodist church. At first he supposed they might be waiting for a wedding or a funeral, but then he noticed that they were all looking upward, while some seemed to be pointing at something in the sky.

He hurried over and joined the group. Then he, too, began looking up. But he couldn't see anything. Only the quaint old shingled steeple, and there was nothing very special about that. He had seen it hundreds of times before, and had watched his daddy climb it more than once.

"What's everybody looking at?" he asked the man standing beside him.

"Can't you see?" said the man, still looking up and pointing.

"See what?" asked Steve.

"The bird."

"Bird?" said Steve. "What bird? I can't see any bird."

"Can't you see that bird tied to the top of the steeple?"

Steve laughed out loud. Who ever heard of a bird tied to the top of a steeple? But he looked again and stopped laughing. The man was right. There *was* a bird up there. And it *was* tied to the top of the steeple.

"Why, it's a young pigeon," he said. "And it's got a piece of string around one of its legs."

"That's right," said the man. "And now tell me how the other end of the string got hooked around something on the steeple."

"I don't know," said Steve. "I suppose it got caught as the bird was flying past the steeple. What a thing to happen!"

By this time more people had joined the group, which was getting so large that it was beginning to block the traffic. Everybody was looking up, watching the poor pigeon trying to break free. It would fly a little way till the string got tight. Then it would fall against the side of the steeple. After much fluttering it would start off again, only to fall once more.

"Poor little bird!" cried someone.

"Somebody get a gun and shoot it!" said another.

"That's right," said a third. "Put the poor thing out of its misery!"

"Oh, no, please don't do that!" said Steve, who loved birds and had always wanted a pigeon for his very own.

"It's the only thing to do," said the man beside him.

"Oh, no!" said Steve. "I'll go up and get it."

"You go up and get it!" laughed the man. "You couldn't do that. It would take a steeplejack to get up there!"

"That's what I'm going to be, some day," said Steve, as he pushed his way through the crowd toward the door of the church.

Fortunately the door was open. Slipping inside, he ran up the stairs, then over to the ladder that led to the trap door which opened onto the roof. Soon he was outside.

Suddenly there was a roar from the crowd below. To the amazement of all, a little boy had appeared on the church roof.

"Come down!" cried somebody with a big voice. "What are you doing up there? Come down!"

But Steve did not come down. Instead, he made his way carefully to the bottom of the steeple. Then, taking off his shoes and socks, he began to climb. Flattened against the steeple, he got a grip and a hold where nobody else would have found one.

Now the eyes of all shifted from the captive pigeon to the little boy.

"Come down! Come down!" shouted half a

"Don't shoot the pigeon," pleaded Steve, *"I'll go up and get it."*

dozen men at once. "You'll fall. You'll break your neck! Come down!"

But Steve did not come down. Instead, with skill he had learned by watching his daddy, he climbed steadily upward, inch by inch, inch by inch. How he held on I do not know. But he did. Stout nails had been left here and there to help the steeplejack, and Steve knew where they were. Keeping his eyes ever upward, and never looking down, he moved slowly but surely toward the place where the string that held the pigeon was caught in a loose shingle.

Meanwhile the crowd had grown till it filled the highway. Policemen had arrived to clear a path for the traffic, only to stop and look up horrified at the little boy perched like a fly on the side of the steeple. One of them blew his whistle and ordered Steve to come down. But Steve never heard.

"He's going to fall! He's going to fall!" cried a lady, and fainted clear away. But Steve knew nothing about it.

"Come down! Come down!" cried one man after another. But still Steve went up, up, up. Little by little. Little by little.

Now he was nearly there. Carefully he reached up and grabbed the string.

Deep silence fell upon the crowd below. Everyone held his breath. Now they were sure he would fall. Surely he couldn't possibly hold on with one hand and tug on the string with the other.

But he did. And to everybody's amazement he didn't just let the string go as he might have done: he started to pull on it!

"Oh, no!" groaned the crowd. "Surely he isn't going to try to catch the bird!"

But that is exactly what Steve did next. Slowly, and with great care, he kept pulling on the string, gradually bringing the bird closer and closer to him. Then he made a grab and the bird was in his hand.

The crowd gasped. Now how could he get down safely with one hand clutching the bird? Surely he was bound to fall to his death.

Then what do you suppose Steve did? Somehow he stuffed that fluttering bird beneath his shirt, buttoned it, and then, with both hands free, began slowly to descend.

Down, down, down he went, while the crowd watched with even greater fear then before.

At last Steve reached the bottom and, quickly slipping on his socks and shoes, ran along the roof to the trapdoor.

As the front door of the church opened and Steve appeared, a mighty cheer went up. Everybody shouted with relief and delight that he was safe and sound. And, of course, everybody wanted to be the first to praise the boy who had so bravely risked his life to save the bird.

When I was told this story by someone who

saw it happen, I could not help but think of Somebody else who risked His life for others. Somebody who climbed, not a steeple, but a cross; Somebody who risked everything to save, not a bird, but boys and girls of every nation.

You know who I mean. And why did He do it? That He might take you and me and everyone and put us close to His heart, and keep us there for ever.

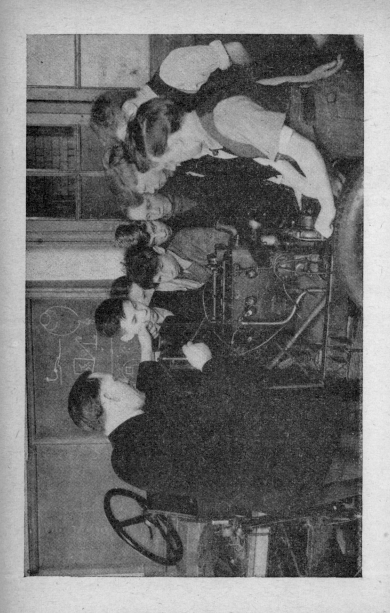

Georgie the Garage Man

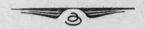

"MAMMA," said Georgie one day, "do you know what I want to be when I grow up?"

"No," said Mamma, "I don't. But I hope you will be a missionary or a doctor, or somebody like that."

"Naw," said Georgie, "nothing like that."

"Then what do you want to be?"

"A garage man," said Georgie.

"A garage man!" said Mamma. "You mean a man who fills cars at petrol stations?"

"No," said Georgie. "I mean a garage man who — er — well, who — er — takes cars apart and puts them together again."

"Oh, I see," said Mamma. "You mean a mechanic."

"I suppose that's the name," said Georgie. "A garage man mechanic."

"But why do you want to be a garage man mechanic?" asked Mamma.

"Oh, I dunno," said Georgie. "I just want to be one, that's all. And could I have a set of garage tools for my birthday?"

PICTURE OPPOSITE: *These fortunate boys have a car in their own classroom which they can practise on.*

Mamma smiled. "Isn't it a little early to buy tools like that? What would you do with them?"

"Oh," said Georgie. "Mend Daddy's car. And Mr. Jones' car. And maybe other people's cars."

Mamma's smile grew broader. "But maybe they wouldn't want a little boy mending their cars."

"Oh, I wouldn't mend their cars unless they really needed it," said Georgie. "And can I have a set of tools for my birthday?"

"We'll see," said Mamma, as mammas so often say.

But when Georgie's birthday arrived, can you guess what he found beside his plate when he came downstairs for breakfast?

Yes! A lovely little set of tools. There were three spanners, a small wrench, a hammer, a screwdriver, and several nuts and bolts and screws.

When Georgie opened the packet and found all these wonderful things inside, he let out one great whoop! and dashed round and round the kitchen holding the three spanners in one hand and the wrench in the other. Then he hugged Mamma and Daddy and little sister, one after the other.

"But now," said Mamma, "these tools are for mending your truck, and little sister's tricycle, and doing odd jobs around the house."

© Fox Photos

PICTURE OPPOSITE: *Georgie decided to be content with his own toy car until he grew older.*

"And for mending cars," said Georgie hopefully.

"No, dear, not unless Daddy asks you to help him."

Georgie seemed a bit disappointed, but it was only for a moment. Then he went back to his box of tools and counted them over and over again.

Then one day Georgie disappeared. Mamma and Daddy simply couldn't find him anywhere. They looked for him all over the house and all over the garden. They went to the house across the road, where Georgie sometimes played with a little boy about his own age. But Georgie was nowhere to be found.

Daddy searched the nearby streets and asked all the people he met if they had seen Georgie anywhere, but it was no use.

On his way back home, where he was going to phone the police, Daddy happened to notice a dark, black stream trickling downhill from underneath a green car that was standing outside his friend Tom Jones' house.

"Strange," he said to himself. "That isn't water, and I don't think it's petrol. But surely it couldn't be oil. Not all that oil."

"Tom!" he called, seeing his friend working in his garden. "I'm afraid there's something the matter with your car. There seems to be an oil leak somewhere."

"It can't be," said Tom. "I had the car serviced only this afternoon."

But he came running out just the same.

"Well, I never did!" he exclaimed. "It *is* oil! Wherever can it be coming from?"

"Sorry I can't stay to help you," said Daddy. "But I'm still looking all over for Georgie. In fact, I was just going indoors to call the police."

Just then there was a movement under the car.

From underneath the mudguard an oily little head poked out.

"I found a nut that was loose," said Georgie, "and I screwed it and screwed it and screwed it, but it didn't screw. It just unscrewed and unscrewed and unscrewed. And then oil started to come all over me. And I tried to put the nut back and it wouldn't go 'cos the oil kept comin' and comin' and comin' and — "

"Georgie!" said Daddy sternly. "What did your mother tell you about using those tools on people's cars? You had better come along with me."

"Oh, but I didn't mean to do any harm," wailed Georgie.

"But you could have done a lot of harm," said Daddy. "There's no excuse for this."

"But," said Mr. Jones, trying not to smile, "if that oil nut was really loose, as it must have been, he may have saved me a bad breakdown."

"Just the same," said Daddy, "I think Mamma will want Georgie to put his garage tools away until he gets old enough to use them wisely."

And Daddy guessed right.

Like Freddie, this little boy has decided that to "love one another" is the best way to be happy.

All Fall Down

MOTHER was out shopping and Daddy was at his office. Otherwise I suppose this strange chapter of accidents would never have happened.

The three children were at home. Freddie was upstairs in his bedroom nailing a picture on the wall. Beverley was busy with pail and mop cleaning the bathroom floor. Little Gwendoline was playing with her blocks in the living room.

For a while everything went along happily. Then, all of a sudden, Beverley heard a sound that sent cold shivers down her spine.

Bump, bump, bump, bumpity bump.

Then there was a piercing shriek.

Jumping to her feet she rushed into the corridor.

"Freddie, did you hear that?" she cried. "It must be Gwendoline. She's fallen down the cellar stairs!"

Like a flash Beverley dashed to the head of the front stairs with only one thought in mind— to get to her little sister as fast as she could. But in her haste she forgot that she had the wet mop still in her hand. Tripping over it, she fell, head over heels, all the way to the bottom.

Bump, bump, bump, bumpity bump!

Poor Beverley!

Meanwhile Freddie, having heard his little sister cry out, had dropped his hammer and run to the back stairs, which were closest to his bedroom. These were very steep stairs and led straight to the kitchen. He had been up and down them a thousand times without any trouble but now, hurrying too fast, he missed his hold on the railing, slipped, sat down hard on the top stair, and, unable to stop, slid all the way down.

Bump, bump, bump, bumpity bump!

Poor Freddie!

Oh, how it hurt! Just where, I leave you to guess. But once at the bottom he didn't stop a moment. Little sister needed him.

Picking himself up, he rushed to the cellar stairs and ran straight into Beverley who was rubbing her forehead and elbow, but also running to help Gwennie. Down the cellar stairs they went together. And together they picked her up. Carefully they felt her all over to make sure no bones were broken, and then carried her up to the living room and set her on the sofa between them.

"Oh, dear!" said Beverley. "I'm afraid I bumped my forehead badly. It hurts an awful lot. So does my elbow."

"Why, what happened to you?" asked Freddie.

"I hurried so to get to Gwennie, I fell all the way down the front stairs."

"Oh, did you?" said Freddie in surprise. "And I fell all the way down the back stairs!"

"Oh, no!" said Beverley. "Not down those steep kitchen stairs! Didn't you get hurt?"

"Oh, yes," said Freddie. "It hurts an awful lot."

"Where?" asked Beverley.

"Well, I can hardly tell you," said Freddie. "But I sat on every one of those stairs very quickly, one after the other."

"Oh," said Beverley, "I suppose that must hurt as much as my head does. We'll just have to love each other an extra lot until all the hurts go away."

And with that they put their arms around each other, with Gwennie in the middle, still sobbing quietly.

Just then the front door opened and Mother came in.

"Well, I never did!" she said. "What in the world has happened? I have never seen all three of you so peaceful before."

Then they told Mother everything, how all three had fallen downstairs almost at the same time, and how they were now just trying to make each other better.

How glad Mother was to find that, despite the bad falls, none of the hurts was serious! But most of all she was thankful for the love that bound them all together, and made them want to help and cheer and comfort each other in time of need.

All children are like stars, and God wants us to shine brightly.

Polishing the Stars

LITTLE Hazel had been in bed quite a long time, but she was not asleep.

Every now and then she would call out, "Mamma, I want to see you," or, "Mamma, I want to ask you something."

But Mamma had heard such things before. She guessed that Hazel was just trying to think of some new excuse to stay awake.

"Go to sleep!" she called.

"But I don't want to go to sleep," said Hazel. "I want you to come and see me."

"Go to sleep!" said Mamma, a little more sternly. "It's long past your bedtime. So, not another word."

For a while there was silence. Then, just as Mamma was telling herself that Hazel was fast asleep, she heard her voice again.

"Mamma, aren't you coming to kiss me good-night?"

"I have kissed you good-night three times already. Now be a good girl and go to sleep."

"But I want to ask you something."

"Oh, dear," said Mamma, to herself. "I suppose I'll have to go."

"Now what is it?" she asked as she entered Hazel's bedroom.

Hazel was sitting up in bed looking out of the window.

"I've got a question I want to ask you, Mamma," she said. "And I can't go to sleep until I know."

"Well, what is it, darling?"

"Is it true, Mamma," said Hazel, "that the angels polish the stars in the daytime so they will shine brightly at night?"

Mamma sat right down on Hazel's bed and laughed.

"Whoever told you such a thing?" she asked.

"The little boy next door," said Hazel. "Isn't it true?"

"Oh, Hazel dear, of course it isn't," said Mamma, smiling. "The stars are great big balls of fire like the sun. Nobody needs to polish them, and nobody could. The only reason they look so small to us is that they are so far away, much farther than the sun."

"But why do they only shine at night?" asked Hazel, looking up in the sky again.

"They don't shine only at night," said Mamma. "They shine all the time—day and night. The only reason we can't see them in the daytime is because the sunshine is so bright. If you were to look up at the sky from the bottom of a deep well, where there is no sunshine, you would see the stars in the daytime all right."

"So the angels don't polish them?" said Hazel a little sadly.

"No," said Mamma. "Of course not. At least, not that kind of star. Maybe, though, they help to polish another kind of star."

"What kind?" asked Hazel.

"Girls and boys," said Mamma, smiling. "They're quite a bit like stars, you know. God told Abraham that he would have children 'like the stars,' and He told Daniel that all the good people will some day shine 'as the stars for ever and ever.'"

"But how can girls and boys be polished?" asked Hazel with a chuckle.

"I can think of a lot of ways," said Mamma. "Their manners, for instance, can stand a lot of polishing—so that they will always be kind to others and respectful to their parents and teachers."

"Do you think I'll shine like the stars some day?" asked Hazel.

"Of course you will, darling," said Mamma, giving her a big hug and kiss. "I think you are shining quite brightly now. And you will shine brighter and brighter as the days go by."

Hazel was satisfied at last. Quickly she snuggled under the bedclothes and went to sleep.

Saved by a Crocodile

SAMBO was one of the brightest boys at the mission school, although, like some other boys I know, he was brighter at play than at work.

He had been attending the school for two or three years, but while many of the other boys had given their hearts to Jesus, Sambo had not. He always wanted to "have a good time," and refused to give up some of the bad habits he had brought with him from his heathen village.

Sometimes the people in charge of the mission had thought of sending Sambo home, but again and again they had forgiven him and let him stay on. Some day, they hoped, something might happen that would lead Sambo to love the Lord.

Despite all his naughty ways, the other boys liked him a great deal, chiefly, perhaps, because he was such a wonderful swimmer. In any sort of race he could leave them all behind, which made him somewhat of a hero.

One afternoon, as they all stood on the bank

© Dorien Leigh

PICTURE OPPOSITE: *"Somebody saw a long, low shape moving toward him."*

of the big, wide river where they went to bathe, one of the boys dared Sambo to swim right across to the other side and back again.

No-one had ever done it before. It was against the rules. Because of the current and the crocodiles, the boys were supposed to stay in their own quiet pool. But you know what boys are, always looking for some new excitement.

And now, as Sambo hesitated, they all began to tease him.

"You're afraid," one said.

"I'm not," said Sambo.

"You couldn't swim that far," said another.

"I could," said Sambo.

"Then why don't you do it?" said a third.

"Maybe I will," said Sambo. "Maybe I will."

But as he did not go in at once, they taunted him some more.

"Let's see you do it!" they cried. "We'll count and see how long you take."

"All right," said Sambo. "I'll try."

"Mind the crocodiles!" cried someone, as Sambo slipped into the water.

"Don't worry about the crocs," he replied. "I can swim faster than they can."

And he was off. With powerful strokes he worked up against the current. Then over toward the middle. While the others held their breath at the daring feat, Sambo drew nearer and nearer to the opposite bank.

At last he stopped swimming and began to

Photo by D. L. Chappell

"Sambo was one of the brightest boys at the mission school."

walk out of the water. At this all the boys clapped their hands and shouted, "Well done, Sambo! Well done!"

For a while Sambo sat on the bank getting his breath for the return trip. Then, as the others watched and shouted to him, he entered the water and began the long swim back.

Then it happened.

Sambo had not been in the water more than two or three minutes when somebody saw a long, low shape moving toward him. It was like a floating tree trunk, but with hard, cruel eyes.

"A crocodile!" he cried.

Then they all saw it and with one accord they yelled, "Look out, Sambo! There's a crocodile right behind you!"

Sambo heard the warning and, looking round, saw the terrible beast coming straight toward him.

He almost leaped out of the water. Never in his life had he swam so fast.

Always he had thought he could outswim a crocodile. But could he? Could he?

Terrified, the others watched the grim race.

For a little while it looked as though Sambo might win. With a great burst of speed he pulled ahead. But no boy alive could keep up such a pace. Gradually the distance narrowed. The crocodile got nearer and nearer.

Suddenly there was a splash, a snap, and poor Sambo disappeared.

With wild cries of fear and sorrow the boys rushed back to the mission.

But when the mission director heard the story he ordered search parties out at once. Crocodiles, he explained, do not eat their prey as soon as they catch it, but bury it until they are ready for their meal. There was just one chance in a hundred, he said, that Sambo might still be alive.

So the search parties started out, combing every yard of both banks of the river, upstream and down.

Meanwhile Sambo, dragged under the water, had lost consciousness. Then, in a narrow inlet hidden by bushes, the crocodile had covered him with mud and sticks and stones, fortunately leaving his head free.

By and by consciousness returned. Sambo awoke to find himself in a crocodile's lair!

You can imagine how frightened he was. He was ready to scream with fear. But at that very moment he remembered something he had been taught in the mission school. He thought about Jesus.

"Jesus!" he cried. "Save me from the crocodile! Please save me from the crocodile! And I will be Thy boy always and always."

Even as he cried out, he heard the tramp of feet. Soon he was looking up into the faces of some of the people from the mission who were searching for him. Quickly they tore away the sticks and rocks, put Sambo on a stretcher, and carried him back to the mission hospital.

To-day, if you were to visit this mission in the heart of Africa, you would meet Sambo. He walks on crutches because of what the crocodile did to his leg. But he doesn't seem to mind. There's a joy on his face that is wonderful to behold. He is one of the finest Christian lads you could wish to meet anywhere in the world.

© Studio Lisa

Donna was greatly disappointed when she saw it was raining.

Donna's Disappointment

THIS story is about a little girl called Donna and a present her mamma bought her.

One evening Mamma told Donna that she had to go out for a little while to see a friend.

"I want to go, too," said Donna.

"Not this evening," said Mamma. "Another time."

"But I want to go with you," said Donna, beginning to cry.

"No," said Mamma, firmly. "I can't take you with me this time. You must stay with Grandma and she will put you to bed."

"But I don't want to stay with Grandma," wailed Donna. "And I don't want to go to bed. I want to go with you."

"I'm sorry, darling," said Mamma. "But you must stay with Grandma this time. And Grandma will be so happy to have you all to herself. What's more, if you are a good girl, I might bring you something nice when I come back."

Donna stopped crying and looked up, interested.

"What will you bring me?" she asked.

"Ah," said Mamma, "it's a secret. But it will

be something very nice indeed. Something you
have wanted for a long time."

"Tell me what it is!" said Donna.

"Not to-night," said Mamma. "But you will
find it beside your bed in the morning. That is,
if Grandma tells me when I get home that you
have been a very, very good girl."

Donna did not reply.

"You *will* be a very good girl with Grandma,
won't you?" said Mamma.

"Yes," said Donna. "And I shall look beside
my bed when I wake up."

Donna tried hard to be a good girl while
Mamma was out. She didn't bother her Grandma
a teeny bit, and when bedtime came she went
right up to bed without even one little grumble.

"What is Mamma going to bring me?" she
asked, as Grandma tucked her in.

"I really don't know," said Grandma. "But
I'm sure it will be a lovely surprise."

And it was.

When Donna awoke in the morning, there
beside her bed was a lovely little watering can. It
was just what she had been coaxing Mamma to
get her for a long, long time. She was so happy
she couldn't get dressed fast enough. Soon she
was in the kitchen, filling the can with water.

"Thank you, thank you, Mamma," she said.
"Now I can go out in the garden and water the
flowers."

Then came her big disappointment.

As she opened the back door to go out into the garden she noticed it was raining.

At first she just stood looking out as though finding it hard to believe her eyes. Then tears began to run down her cheeks. She put down the watering can and turned to Mamma.

"Didn't God know that you bought me a watering can and that I wanted to water the flowers?" she said, fretfully.

Mamma picked her up in her arms and tried to kiss the tears away.

"Yes, God knew," she said. "God knows everything. But sometimes, darling, He has to teach us to be patient, doesn't He?"

"But I wanted to use my watering can."

"I know, dear," said Mamma. "But you will still have your watering can when the rain is over. And the flowers will still be there. And they will need more water later on. And, don't forget, dear, your tiny watering can will only water your own little garden. It couldn't possibly water all the other people's gardens, and the farms where the corn and potatoes grow. God has to look after them, too, and that's why He sends the rain."

Donna wasn't quite sure about it, and looked sadly down at her canful of water.

"I suppose I'll have to wait," she said.

"That's a good girl," said Mamma. "Soon the sun will shine again."

And it did. And then Donna watered and watered and watered to her heart's content.

Randy's Lost Ball

SOMEBODY had just given Randy a new ball, and was he happy! It wasn't too big and it wasn't too small, but just the right size for his little hands to hold and throw. And he threw it. All over the place.

Tossing it high in the air he would let it bounce a few times. Then he would run after it, catch it, and toss it up in the air again. What fun it was!

Then one afternoon Mamma called him indoors for some thing or other, and he forgot to take his ball with him.

When he went out into the garden again he saw two strange boys playing with it. They were big boys, about ten years old, so Randy, who was much younger and smaller, didn't dare to say anything. He just watched them as they threw his precious ball to each other.

By and by the two boys thought of a new game and began tossing the ball over the tool shed. One boy stayed in the garden and the other went into the field beyond the shed, and back and forth they threw the ball.

They kept this up for some time, and then

suddenly the throwing stopped. Randy wondered
what was the matter. He soon found out, for the
boy in the field came round from behind the shed
and said, "I couldn't find it." Then, believe it
or not, the two boys just walked away.

Poor Randy was heart-broken. Rushing indoors he cried, "Mamma! They've lost my ball!
They've lost my ball!"

"Who have?" asked Mamma.

"Those two boys. They threw it over the shed
and it's lost."

"Don't worry," said Mamma. "I'll come and
help you find it."

But this was easier said than done. The grass
in the field behind the shed was tall and thick, and
the ball was nowhere to be found. Mamma and
Randy tramped all over the field, up and down,
up and down, up and down, but still they couldn't
find it. Daddy joined them, and he couldn't find
it either. The ball had just disappeared.

Randy went to bed that night a very sad little
boy. But in the morning he made up his mind to
try again. So he went out to that field once more
and searched and searched. But it was no use.
Still he could not find his ball.

Now Mamma had been reading to Randy
from *Uncle Arthur's Bedtime Stories* about some
of the wonderful answers to prayer that other
children have had. So he kept saying to Mamma,
"Why don't we ask Jesus to help us find the ball?"

But Mamma said, "You see, Randy, a ball is such a little thing. We shouldn't trouble Jesus about anything like that."

But Randy didn't think his ball was too little for Jesus. He had great faith. Every day he asked Mamma to pray, even though she didn't do it, and kept putting him off. And every day he went out into the field and looked for his ball.

After five days Randy said, "Mamma, why don't you pray and ask Jesus to help me find my ball? Let's pray right now."

"Very well, dear," said Mamma. "If you want it so badly, we'll pray; but you mustn't be disappointed if you still don't find your ball. God doesn't say 'Yes' every time we pray. It wouldn't be good for us if He did."

"Maybe," said Randy, "but I believe He is going to answer our prayer this time."

So they knelt down and prayed. First, Randy. Then Mamma. By and by they got to their feet. Then Randy said—and these are his very words —"All right, Mamma, now you go and get my ball."

It was almost too much for Mamma. For a moment she did not know what to do. Then she walked out of the house and over to the field behind the shed.

And this is what happened, just as she told me about it: "I started out," she said, "walking at an angle through the tall grass. I had not gone twenty feet when I leaned over and picked up the ball for which we had searched so long. To me it was a direct answer to a prayer. How wonderful to have a God who can hear a little boy asking for a lost ball!"

I think so, too. So does Randy.

Happy is the girl or boy who has a faithful dog for a friend.

Faithful Rover

SCHOOL was out, and all the children of the village were having the happiest time playing in a huge pile of sand someone had dumped on a vacant plot.

Running from one to another, and barking loudly in sheer delight, was Rover, the children's special friend. A large, beautiful dog, with a shiny black coat, he was known and loved by every boy and girl for miles around. He loved them, too, letting them pet him and comb him any time they wished, and romping with them in the friendliest way whenever they came out to play.

Suddenly there was a cry of alarm. The children stopped playing and stood still, seemingly rooted to the ground.

"Mad dog! Mad dog!" somebody was shouting. "Look out for the mad dog!"

Then someone else cried, "Run children, run, there's a mad dog coming!"

Then they saw it, an ugly beast, foaming at the mouth, and coming toward them with great leaps and bounds. Running behind it was a man with a gun, afraid to shoot lest he hit one of the children.

"Run!" he cried to them, "run!"

They ran. But, alas, not all in the same direction. Some started to run one way, some another, until they were all mixed up and falling over each other in their fright.

Another moment and the mad dog would have been upon them. But it never reached them.

Suddenly a black form streaked past the children and hurled itself at the mad dog. It was Rover, risking his own life for his little pals.

For a moment it seemed as though there would be a terrible fight. But there was not. Instead, the mad dog gave one great leap into the air and, in a final spasm of pain, fell to the ground. At this the man with the gun ran up and shot it.

Now the children came running back to find out what had happened to Rover. How thankful they were to discover that he was unhurt!

But as they went to pat and stroke him as before, the neighbours held them back.

"No," they said; "Rover may have been bitten by the mad dog. If so, he may go mad himself. He will have to be killed, too."

You should have seen those children then!

"You mustn't shoot our Rover!" they cried. "We won't let you shoot him. He's our dog. He won't go mad!"

Then some of the girls began to cry, and first one, then another pleaded, "Please don't shoot Rover. Please, please, let him live. He's our friend, our best friend."

What with one and another begging that Rover's life be spared, the neighbours at last agreed not to shoot him. But to make quite sure that he would not go mad like the other dog, they insisted that he be tied up for a month. If at the end of that time he was all right, they said, he could go free again.

So this is what they did. Rover was tied to a tree with a strong rope, inside a fence, and left there to see what would happen to him. But the children did not forget him. No, indeed! They came to see him whenever they could, bringing him all sorts of nice things to eat. He never was treated so well in all his life.

And the children were right. Rover didn't go mad. When the month was up he was set free, and came back to romp and play with them as before.

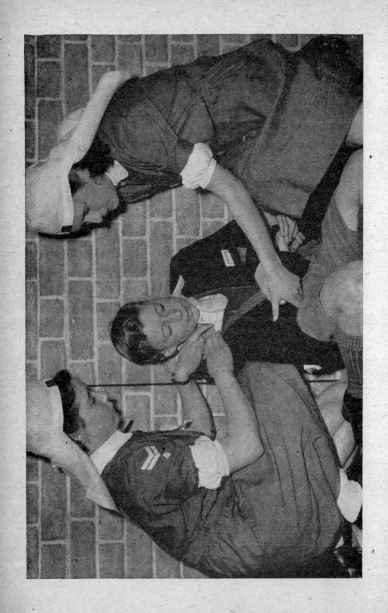

The Wrong Medicine

NOT long ago I stayed for a night in a little mountain cottage. I hadn't been there long when there was a knock on my door. When I opened it I saw two of the nicest, happiest little boys one could ever wish to see. They looked like two plump little cherubs.

They said their names were Rob and Lyn, and they had just come to see me. So I said I was very glad to see them. And I was just wondering what to say next when I noticed that one of them had a great big scar on his fine, manly face, as though he had been badly burned some time or other.

"However did that happen?" I asked, trying to be friendly. "Whatever have you been doing to yourself?"

Then they told me the story together, each one adding some point that the other forgot.

"We were playing doctor and patient," said Rob, the bigger of the two.

PICTURE OPPOSITE: *It is fun to play at doctors and patients, but don't make Joyce's mistake.*

"I was the doctor," said Lyn, the younger, "and he was the patient. Our daddy is a doctor, you know."

"But what happened?" I asked.

"Well, we played that Rob had got hurt some way. I'm not sure where he got hurt. I think it was his leg. But he was hurt, anyway."

"And Lyn took me to see Ken," said Rob. "He's a friend of ours, and he has a chemistry set."

"Yes," said Lyn. "And he said he would give us some medicine to make Rob better."

"That's right," said Rob. "And then Joyce and her friend came along. They are girls we play with sometimes. Joyce said she would be the nurse and give me the medicine."

"Then Ken began mixing the medicine," said Lyn. "He said it was only salt and water, but it would make Rob's leg better."

"But I never got that medicine," said Rob.

"Why not?" I said.

"Because Joyce got excited and picked up another bottle," said Lyn. "It was a different one, and she never noticed."

"And it didn't have a cork in it," said Rob. "So when I tipped it up it spilled on my cheek. And then I yelled."

"You should have heard him yell," said Lyn.

"Whatever was in the bottle?" I asked.

"Some sort of acid," said Rob. "And it burned and burned and burned."

"Ken guessed what it was," said Lyn, "and he started looking for soda to put on it."

"And Joyce ran for our daddy," said Rob. "And he came running."

"And he started shouting for soda, too," said Lyn.

"Anyway, he bathed it," said Rob, "and by and by it didn't hurt quite so much."

"How long ago did it happen?" I asked.

"About four months," said Rob. "And my daddy says he's going to graft some new skin on the scar some day so it won't show any more."

"That's fine!" I said. "I'm sure he'll make it quite better. But to think you had all this pain and trouble just because somebody gave you the wrong medicine!"

"Yes," said Rob, wisely. "And my daddy says we should be very careful never to play with bottles when we don't know what's inside them."

"How right he is!" I said.

And I hope every boy and girl who reads this story will remember the lesson from what happened to Rob.

© Studio Lisa

Richard learned that the only way to succeed was to make thorough preparation.

All Over Again

RICHARD came home from school looking very blue.

"What's the matter?" asked Daddy.

"Failed!" said Richard.

"Failed in what?" asked Daddy.

"Arithmetic," said Richard in disgust. "Got to take the exam all over again."

"Well, what happened? Why did you fail?"

"I suppose I didn't give the teacher as many apples and flowers as the other boys did."

"I don't think it's a matter of apples and flowers," said Daddy. "There's another reason."

"What?" asked Richard.

"Preparation," said Daddy, "or the lack of it."

"Well, don't I study?" said Richard. "Don't I study as much as the others do?"

"Maybe so," said Daddy, "but not as much as you need to. As I've told you a dozen times, you play too much and study too little."

"Who wants to study, anyway?" said Richard, walking off in a huff.

"Oh, just a minute, Richard," said Daddy.

"I want you to help me with a little job for a few minutes."

"What is it?" asked Richard suspiciously.

"Mixing some concrete. You know, we have to relay that slab outside the back door that cracked all to pieces the other day."

"O.K.," said Richard. "Let's get it over."

They mixed the concrete just outside the garage. Daddy shovelled in the gravel and Richard the cement.

"Let's not forget the formula," said Daddy. "Three parts of gravel and one of cement."

"Why do we have to be so particular?" said Richard.

"Because that's the way to make good concrete," said Daddy.

"Why don't we put in ten parts of gravel and only one of cement? Wouldn't that save money?"

"It would save money to start with," said Daddy, "but we would soon have to do the job all over again. So it would cost us more in the end. In fact, the only reason why we have to do this job now is because somebody did a poor job before. Probably the person who made that slab outside the back door never bothered to measure the amount of gravel and cement he put in, or he didn't mix it properly, or he made it too wet. Somewhere in the process he didn't make the right preparation. And that's why it all broke to pieces and we have to do the job again."

"Are you trying to tell me something about

getting ready for examinations?" said Richard
with a sly grin.

"Why, Richard," said Daddy, grinning back
at him, "whatever made you think that?"

"Oh, it just sounded like it," said Richard.

"Funny," said Daddy. "The fact is that mixing concrete and getting ready for exams are very
much alike. To prepare for exams you have to
put in just the right amount of study and the
right amount of play. Otherwise you'll never
succeed. About three to one, I would say. The
study will get your mind ready for the exam, and
the play will help to keep you in good trim. If
you put in too much play and too little study, the
result won't stand the test of time—or of exams."

"I guess I didn't put in the proper amounts
last time," said Richard.

"But you can try again," said Daddy.

"I surely will," said Richard. "And next time
the mixture will be right."

© Studio Lisa.

Patsy showed her forgiving spirit when playing rounders with Monica and the other girls.

Not On Purpose

PATSY, one of the nicest girls in school, was sitting on a bench in the playground with her legs stretched out in front of her as she talked to one of her friends.

All of a sudden a group of girls ran by. One of them, tripping over Patsy's legs, fell heavily to the ground. When she got up she was very angry.

"You nasty, mean thing!" she said. "You tripped me up on purpose!"

"I didn't, really I didn't, Monica," said Patsy. "It was an accident. I'm very sorry."

"It wasn't an accident," said Monica, sharply. "I know you. You hate me and that's why you did it."

"I don't hate you. Really I don't," said Patsy gently. "I wasn't even thinking about you."

"I'll get my own back, I will," said Monica. "You wait and see."

Seeing the crowd that had gathered, and wondering what all the hubbub was about, a teacher strolled up.

"Now what's the trouble?" she asked.

"Patsy tripped me up," said Monica angrily. "On purpose, too."

"Really, Miss, I didn't," said Patsy. "I just had my legs stuck out too far, I suppose, and she fell over them. It was just an accident."

Teacher knew the two girls well.

"Monica," she said, "if Patsy says she didn't do it on purpose, you should accept it. She had no reason for tripping you up, and you shouldn't accuse her of doing so. Many times things that seem to have been done 'on purpose' are just pure accident."

Monica turned away, grumbling to herself about "getting even with her some day," and the crowd broke up. Soon everybody had forgotten all about the incident.

Two or three days later, however, they had reason to remember it.

The girls were playing rounders. Patsy was batting and hit the ball along the ground. Monica picked it up and threw it in as hard as she could. But it was a bad throw, and the ball hit Patsy a nasty crack on the head.

"Oh!" shouted Patsy, trying her best not to cry.

The players crowded round to see how badly she was hurt.

"That's Monica for you," said someone. "The mean thing, trying to get her own back!"

"I wasn't!" shouted Monica. "I didn't mean to hit her."

"Yes, you did. You did it on purpose," retorted another.

"I didn't!" she said hotly. "It was an accident. The ball didn't go straight."

Then Patsy showed her greatness.

"It's all right, Monica," she said. "I'm sure it was an accident. I know you didn't mean to hurt me. And I'm sure you wouldn't have done it on purpose."

Suddenly Monica remembered. It all came back to her. All those unkind things she had said to Patsy just a day or two ago.

"It's very kind of you to say so," she said. "And really, Patsy, it was an accident, I assure you."

"I'm sure it was," said Patsy, trying to smile as she rubbed the sore place on her head.

The other girls started to go back to their places in the game, feeling that something very fine had happened.

And it had. Patsy had shown a beautiful spirit of forgiveness and Monica had learned that oftentimes things that seem to be done on purpose are really only accidents after all.

From that day on the two girls were the best of friends and never quarrelled again.

"Daddy decided to take all the family up to the lake for a picnic,"

The
Purse that Wouldn't Sink

YOU have probably read the story in the Bible about the iron axe head that floated. That was very wonderful, and I can't explain how it happened. But I can tell you a story like it—about the purse that wouldn't sink.

It was a beautiful day, with brilliant sunshine and not a cloud in sight, so Daddy decided to take all the family up to the lake for a picnic. Some friends went along, too, so it made a very happy party.

As soon as a nice spot to camp had been found, Daddy and the older boys went to the boathouse and hired a rowing boat. In no time at all they were out on the lake, rowing for all they were worth. When they got tired they made for the sandy beach where the ladies were busy getting the meal ready.

Jumping out of the boat, Daddy and the boys anchored it securely and hurried over to the fire where some very nice-smelling things were cooking. Hungry as could be, they were very pleased to find such a good meal on the way. Mamma hadn't seen Daddy so happy for a long time.

Then something happened that spoiled everything. Daddy started feeling in his trousers pockets. Then he picked up his coat and felt through its pockets.

"Looking for something?" asked Mamma.

"Yes," he said, with a worried look creeping over his face. "My purse. I seem to have mislaid it. I am sure I brought it with me."

"Yes, you did," said one of the boys. "You had it in your hand when you paid for the boat."

"Of course," said Daddy. "Of course. But where did I put it?"

"Maybe you dropped it in the boat when you took your coat off," said Mamma.

"Perhaps I did," said Daddy, with a look of relief.

"Let's look in the boat."

They did. All of them. Never was a boat searched more carefully by so many people. But the purse was not there.

As they walked back to the fire Mamma whispered, "Did you have much money in it?"

"Yes," said Daddy. "That's what is worrying me. I had all my money in it."

"Oh, dear!" said Mamma. "That's terrible. I hope you find it. We couldn't afford to lose all that."

"But where do we look next?" said Daddy helplessly.

"You could have left it at the boathouse," said someone.

"That's right," said Daddy, "I might have done. I'll go and see."

So Daddy walked back to the boathouse, but the boatman said he hadn't seen it, and nobody had reported finding it.

Sadly Daddy returned to the others.

By the time he got back to the camp site the ladies were all in the boat, and the boys were pushing it off.

"Did you find it?" Mamma called from the bow of the boat.

"No, not a sign," said Daddy.

"I'll be praying," said Mamma.

"I'm afraid it's not much use," he said. Yet he prayed, too.

The lake was smooth as glass, the only ripples being made by passing boats. Mamma and the others enjoyed their trip immensely, their happiness marred only by the thought that poor Daddy was so worried about his lost purse.

The sun was sinking now and the lake was becoming more and more beautiful as the glorious shades of sunset were reflected in its calm waters.

By and by the wonderful stillness was broken by the toot of a large motor launch that seemed to be coming straight toward them. Crowded with passengers, its flags and banners made a gay sight. As it drew near, it veered off to the right and the little rowing boat went bouncing over the waves that it left behind.

Suddenly a dark object appeared on the crest of a wave. It was squarish, and oddly familiar.

I don't know who saw it first, but someone said, "Look at that strange thing in the water! Whatever is it?"

Now they were all looking, and it seemed that each wave was bringing the object nearer.

As it came close to the boat, Mamma reached over the side and picked it up.

"It's Daddy's purse!" she cried excitedly.

Then she opened it and looked for the money. The notes were all there. Very wet, it is true, but, as far as she could see, none was missing.

How the ladies rowed to the shore! When they drew near the beach, where Daddy was waiting for them, they shouted together, "We've found it! We've found it!"

"Found what?" shouted Daddy.

"Your purse," cried Mamma, holding it up. Daddy could hardly believe his eyes.

"But why didn't it sink?" he said, when he felt how wet and heavy it was.

"I just don't know," said Mamma. "It is all very wonderful."

And when they told the boatman, he was astonished. Holding the soggy purse in his hands he said, "It's nothing short of a miracle. It's an act of God."

Daddy and Mamma thought so, too.

How Johnnie Got Wet

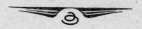

MISS Gibson was marking the register.

"Everybody seems to be in school on time to-day," she said. "That is, all except Johnnie. Has anybody seen Johnnie?"

No-one spoke.

"Does anybody know if Johnnie is ill?"

A hand went up.

"He can't be ill, Miss Gibson, for I saw him fishing in the river yesterday evening."

"Thank you," said Miss Gibson, closing the book. "And now, I'll be back in just a moment. Please, all of you, be good and quiet until I return."

Teacher had barely walked across the corridor, however, when the classroom door opened, and in walked Johnnie.

Immediately bedlam broke loose.

"Johnnie!" cried one of the boys. "What have you been doing?"

"Johnnie!" cried another, "what a mess you're in! Where have you been?"

They had reason to ask. For never had a boy come to school quite like this. Johnnie was actu-

ally dripping wet. His hair was all tousled as if
he had been swimming. His clothes were sodden,
and his shoes squelched water as he walked.

"Ha! Ha! Ha!" laughed everybody. "He!
He! He!" "What a sight!" "What a way to come
to school!"

Suddenly the door handle rattled. Instantly
there was silence. Johnnie moved swiftly to his
desk and sat down.

Teacher entered and looked around.

"So you are here at last, Johnnie," she said.
"Have you any excuse for being late?"

"Well — er — no. I don't think so."

"What do you mean, 'I don't think so'? Have
you, or haven't you, an excuse?"

"I s'pose I haven't," said Johnnie.

"What has happened to your hair?" asked
Teacher.

"Nothing, Miss," said Johnnie, trying in vain
to make it go into place.

"Stand up!" said Teacher.

Johnnie stood up.

A hand was raised.

"Please, Miss, there's a puddle under Johnnie's
seat."

At this laughter broke out all over the classroom.

"Silence!" said Miss Gibson.

"Johnnie, come here! Why are you so wet?"

"Well — er — " began Johnnie.

Just what he was going to say next nobody

knows, for just then the door opened again, and this time the headmaster walked in.

"Do you have a boy here called Johnnie Gordon?" he asked. "The police—"

"The police!" whispered all the children.

"There he is," said Miss Gibson.

"The police," said the headmaster, "have just phoned up to ask about him. They say he jumped off the bridge on his way to school this morning and saved the life of a little girl who had fallen into the river and was drowning. Are you the boy?" he said, turning to Johnnie.

"Yes, sir, please, sir."

"I'm proud of you, son. That was a brave thing to do. God bless you. But why didn't you go back home to change?"

"I was afraid my Dad would be angry with me for getting my clothes soaked," said Johnnie.

"Well, he's *not* angry with you," said the headmaster. "I've talked with him. He's as proud of you as I am." Then, turning to the class, "We're all proud of him, aren't we, children?"

Suddenly everybody was cheering. And the very ones who had been laughing at Johnnie a few minutes before, cheered the loudest. How wonderful it seemed to have a real hero right in their own classroom!

And soon the whole town was talking of the brave little boy who saved a girl from drowning on his way to school and was too modest to let anybody know about it.

© Keystone

A farm is a wonderful place for fun, but poor May paid dearly for her mistake.

Trouble in the Hayloft

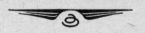

MAY lived on a farm in Texas with her daddy and mamma and nine brothers and sisters.

What a family! And what fun they all had together! With horses to ride, cows to milk, calves and colts to look after, chickens to feed, and dogs and cats to play with, there was never a dull moment for anybody.

Sometimes the children would all get together in the big barn and start jumping from the hayloft onto the big pile of hay below. They would climb up the tall ladder like squirrels and jump off the top over and over again.

Then one of the boys hurt himself. Not badly, but just enough to make Daddy put a stop to it all, in case one of the others might get hurt worse. He said there was to be no more jumping from the hayloft, ever. And when Daddy spoke firmly like that the children all knew he meant what he said.

Of course, as you can imagine, they didn't like it a bit, for they had played in the hayloft as long as they could remember. Some were quite upset, especially May, the ten-year-old. She couldn't see why everybody had to stop jumping just because one of the boys had hurt himself a little bit. But she obeyed, like the rest, until— well, until one afternoon some visitors arrived with a couple of children about May's age.

While the four parents went indoors to chat, May, with some of her brothers and sisters, made friends with the two little guests. By and by May asked them if they would like to see around the farm, and of course they said yes. So they started off together, and pretty soon they came to the big barn.

"What a lovely place to play!" cried the two visitors. "It's so much bigger than ours. Don't you have lots of fun jumping from the hayloft?"

"Well, yes," said May. "We used to before Daddy said we mustn't."

"Why don't we jump now?" said the two visitors. "We've got lots of time and *our* parents won't mind."

May and the others kept silent. They wanted to go up into the hayloft just as much as the others, but they kept thinking of what Daddy had told them.

"Come on," said the two little girls, as they went up the ladder. "Why don't you come?"

May looked at the others and then followed them.

"I think it will be all right, just for this afternoon," she said.

So up she went.

Some of the others climbed up, too, and soon they were all having the grandest time jumping off onto the hay.

Then it happened. I am not sure just what May did. Perhaps she slipped. I don't know. But whatever the cause, she missed the main pile of hay and landed on the concrete floor.

The others were horrified and came running to where May lay unconscious.

At any other time they would have run to tell Daddy, but now they didn't dare. They all knew they had been disobedient and were afraid of what he might say to them. As for the two visitors, they were in tears. "It was all our fault!" they said.

After a while, two of the boys decided they had better take May to the house anyway. So they picked her up, and were just going out of the barn door, when May began to recover.

"Don't take me indoors!" she cried. "Daddy will be so angry. Please don't tell Daddy."

They helped her to stand up, but she was very dizzy. Then she began to cry and plead with them to keep it all secret, and they agreed. Daddy was never told, nor Mamma. Not till years afterward.

But sometimes Daddy and Mamma wondered what had happened to May. She was a changed girl, so different from the girl she had been before that fateful afternoon. She was always complaining of headaches. And always tired. How much she suffered!

They took her to the doctor time and again. He gave her medicine of one kind and another, but none of it did her any good. As she got worse instead of better, he decided to give her a thorough examination, with X-rays and all the rest. And that is when he found the fracture. Then, of course, the truth came out.

May had to have a serious operation before she got better. All because of one act of disobedience which she was afraid to confess.

To-day May is grown up and has children of her own. I met her the other day. She told me how she tells this story from her childhood to her own boys and girls to teach them to obey, and tell the truth, and never to cover up a wrong.

News for Mamma

ARE you always very good and quiet when you go to church? I hope so.

Such a lot of children don't seem to know how they should act in a place of worship. They wriggle, and whisper, and fuss, and drop things on the floor, and even walk about during the service just as though they were in a school play-ground.

I remember having to stop in the middle of a sermon one day because a little girl was wandering up and down the centre aisle of the church, trying to make everybody look at her. She was succeeding only too well. So I said, "There seems to be a little girl here who has lost her mamma." Her mamma found her, pretty quickly.

Sometimes I have seen a daddy take a little boy in his arms out of a meeting, and from certain sounds that came back through the open church door I gathered somebody was getting a lesson on how to behave in the house of God.

And that brings me to the story of Dickie. Such a dear little boy he was, when he was good. But in church—oh, dear!

Mamma had done her best to make him under-stand that a church is a place where people go to meet God and everyone should be very quiet and reverent. But Dickie either couldn't, or wouldn't, see why he should be any different in church than in his own garden.

Then one day there was a very important service that Mamma wanted to attend. And she simply had to take Dickie because everybody else wanted to go, too, and there was nobody at home with whom she could leave him.

To make quite sure that all would be well, she gave Dickie a good talking to beforehand, making it very plain to him how important it was that he should be specially good at this very special meeting.

And he was, for a while. Then he began to fidget.

Mamma gave him a piece of paper and a pencil.

Pretty soon Dickie dropped the pencil and it ran under the next pew.

"Be still!" whispered Mamma.

"I want a drink," said Dickie.

"You can't have a drink till the meeting's over," said Mamma. "So be a good boy."

Dickie sat up straight and seemed as though he was going to obey. Eagerly Mamma turned her eyes toward the preacher, hoping to get his next point, but alas, it was not to be.

"I want to go home!" said Dickie, loudly.

"Ssh!" whispered Mamma. "Be quiet!"

"But I want to go home!" said Dickie.

"You can't go home now," said Mamma.
"Here, take this," she said, passing Dickie her
handbag, usually good for ten minutes' peace.

For a few minutes it was effective. Dickie
probed this precious box of mysteries to the
bottom, bringing forth all Mamma's private things
for the other churchmembers to view. Then he
let the handbag drop with a loud clatter.

This was too much for Mamma. At first she
thought she would take him out, but changed
her mind because she did so want to hear the rest
of the sermon. Then she put both arms round
Dickie, gripped him firmly, lifted him up a little
way, and sat him down hard on the pew.

For a full minute there was complete silence.
Quite clearly, Dickie had had a big surprise.

By and by he leaned over toward Mamma and
began to whisper.

"What is it now?" said Mamma.

"Mamma," said Dickie, "I have news for
you."

It was all Mamma could do not to smile. But
the minister seemed to be looking right at her,
so she kept her face straight.

"What news?" she whispered.

"I'm going to be good in church after this,"
said Dickie, his face pious as a cherub's.

"Good!" whispered Mamma fervently, but
doubtfully.

"I am," said Dickie, "really."

And, believe it or not, he was.

© Keystone

Like Marie, this lucky little girl has two dogs for her pets.

Two Dogs and a Girl

THE two dogs were Teddy and Blackie.

Teddie was almost all white, but had two black ears and one black front paw. Blackie was black all over.

The girl was Marie. Quite little, she was very sweet and dear, and very much loved by her mamma and daddy and auntie, and all the neighbours, and, well, by everybody who knew her.

Not far from where Marie lived there flowed a fairly wide river, which was quite deep in places. Here, every morning, Teddy and Blackie would run for a swim. Sometimes Mamma and Daddy and Marie would go along, too, just to watch the two dogs having fun together in the water.

Marie, of course, was never allowed to go to the river alone, but one day, as she saw the two dogs racing off for their morning dip, she decided to follow them.

Right down to the river bank she went, and then on into the water after them. If Mamma and Daddy had known what she was up to, they would have had the fright of their lives for, only a little way from the bank, the river bottom dropped away steeply.

They were frightened enough when they discovered that Marie was nowhere about the house. First they looked for her in the garden, where she loved to play. Then they inquired of the neighbours. But none of them had seen or heard the little girl.

While they were standing on their front lawn wondering what to do next, and getting more and more worried every minute, Teddy, his curly white coat soaking wet, came running up the road, barking madly. Then he turned round and started running back to the river.

Thinking that something must be the matter, Daddy started to run after Teddy, and Mamma followed him. Then Auntie ran, too, and all the neighbours who had been talking to them on the lawn.

When they got to the river, what do you suppose they saw?

There, several feet from the bank, and only a foot or so from the sharp drop in the river bottom, stood Marie, laughing and splashing merrily. Beside her was Blackie *with her overall straps in his mouth*, keeping her from walking any farther into the stream.

You can imagine what happened next. Daddy rushed into the water and picked up Marie, while Mamma and Auntie and the other people became so excited they were half crying and half laughing all the way back home.

As for Teddy and Blackie, they got more

© Fox Photos

Blackie, and his brother Teddy, got more petting than they had had in all their lives.

petting and patting than they had had in all their lives.

"That was the best piece of joint life-saving I've seen for a long time," said Daddy, after it was all over. "How in the world did Teddy know he should run back to fetch us while Blackie held on to Marie?"

Nobody could answer. Nor can I. Unless, maybe, dogs can talk to each other, just as we do, in their own doggy way.

Tom loved to go fishing

When Tom Went Fishing

TOM lived in a house beside a river. In fact, his house was built so close to the river bank that it was set on piles so that it wouldn't be washed away should the tide rise too high some day. He could look out of his bedroom window and watch boats going by just a few feet away from him.

Lucky boy! you say? He surely was.

And how he loved the water! He could swim like a fish, and row a small boat like an old sailor. But most of all he loved to go fishing. In fact, he loved to fish so much that often his mother had quite a time of it trying to get him to do anything else. Whenever the tide was right, off he wanted to go with his fishing rod, never mind the weather, or how many jobs were waiting for him at home.

One chilly autumn afternoon Mamma really put her foot down—hard.

"No fishing to-day," she said, as Tom began to plead. "That biting wind will give you a death of cold."

"Phooey!" said Tom. "I'm not afraid of the cold. And there'll be a dozen boys down at the bridge. They don't mind when it's cold, Ma. Not if they're catching fish."

"But I mind," said Mamma. "You are not going fishing to-day. Anyway, you haven't lifted a finger to help me all this week. It's just fishing, fishing, fishing, till I'm tired of it."

"Oh, but Ma, the bass are coming in and some of the boys have caught some already. Big ones. I might catch a big one this afternoon. Please let me go."

"Not to-day, Tom," said Mamma firmly. "There's the piano. You haven't played a note since last Wednesday. And you know your teacher said you were to practise at least half an hour a day."

"Who wants to play the mouldy old piano when the bass are coming in?" grumbled Tom, pouting.

"All the same," said Mamma firmly, "half an hour's practice right now is what you are going to do."

"Oh, no, Ma! Not right now!" Tom almost shrieked. "Why, the tide's just on the turn, and that's the best time to catch fish."

"It will have to turn to-day without you," said Mamma. "Now let me hear that piano."

Tom sat down on the piano stool. But he didn't have very much music in him just then. He tried to look at the notes in the book, but his eyes kept wandering out of the window at the water swirling by.

Most sensible people would have been glad to stay indoors on such an afternoon, for the sky was cloudy and the chill wind was whipping up the grey water into quite large waves. But not Tom. To him it was all beautiful. And especially at the turn of the tide.

By and by, as he thumped away at the piano, he thought he noticed a strange stillness in the house. He stopped playing and listened.

He was right. Mamma had gone out. He was alone. Now was his chance!

Quickly he slipped on his jacket, opened the back door, and ran down the steps to where he kept his fishing rod and a bottle of worms. He found them in their usual place, amid the piling under the house. A moment later he was running at top speed for the bridge.

As he had guessed, there were several other boys there already, all well wrapped up against the chilly wind and eagerly watching their lines.

It didn't take Tom long to bait his hook and get ready to throw his line in beside the others.

But it never got there.

Suddenly he gave an unearthly shriek.

"Oh, my finger!" he yelled. "The hook's got caught in my finger!"

It had indeed. In the third finger of his left hand.

The other boys propped up their rods as best they could and ran over to see what had happened.

"It's gone right in!" said one.

Tom preferred fishing to reading or playing the piano.

"Never get it out," said another. "The barb will keep it from coming."

"Only thing to do is to push it all the way through," said a third.

"Oh, no!" cried Tom, letting out another yell. "Oh, no! Don't do that! I won't let you! I won't! Stop it!"

"All right, then," said one of the older boys who was trying his best to remove the hook. "Someone take him to the doctor. If he won't let us push it out it will have to be cut out. And it had better be soon or he'll lose his finger altogether."

The very thought made Tom yell again. But there was nothing else to do now. To the doctor he had to go. And just as the big boy had said, the doctor had to cut the hook out.

Poor Tom! How it hurt! Oh, how he wished Mamma were there to comfort him!

Mamma! He had forgotten her till now. Of course, she didn't know anything about it. She thought he was playing the piano. What would she say when she found out?

He didn't have long to wait to learn that. When he got home Mamma said a lot.

And that was the end of Tom's fishing, for quite a long time. But he told me that the lesson he learned that day stayed with him for years. He never disobeyed his mother again, whether the tide was on the turn or not.

This little girl loves birds, and the birds love her.

Birds in the Bedroom

ROGER, Sid and their little sister June lived in a quaint old house on the banks of a lovely stream. It was a beautiful place and the three children were the happiest youngsters for miles around. From sunrise to sundown their shouts of joy and happy laughter mingled with the merry songs of hundreds of birds in the trees about them.

One of the things they liked to do most was to build bird houses and watch the robins, sparrows, blue-tits, and the rest squabbling over which should live in them.

Once Roger cut a hole in a gallon oil can and nailed it to a post to see what would happen. Imagine his surprise when a pair of beautiful robins took possession of it right away!

Then one day all the fun was spoiled. The three children went down with measles, one after the other. First June, then Sid, and finally Roger. Mamma put them all to bed in the same room to save work. But worst of all she kept the blind down all day lest the light should hurt their eyes. So they couldn't see anything that was going on outside, nor even watch their bird boxes.

It was a sad time for everybody, even though Mamma did her best to keep them all happy in one way or another. But by and by Mamma had read every storybook in the house, and told every story she had ever heard. What to do next to amuse them she did not know.

Roger, Sid, and June soon became tired of being in bed, and wanted to get up and play in the garden again. But Mamma said they mustn't, or they might get worse. So they lay in bed and grumbled and grumbled and grumbled, just as most people do when they are beginning to get better from an illness.

Then one day, just when Mamma had finished the last story, and couldn't think of anything else to say or do to please her restless patients, a visitor arrived.

He came in, uninvited, through the front door. But he didn't walk in. He flew in. And he perched on the dressing table in the bedroom where the three sick children were lying.

The funny thing was, he didn't take any notice of Roger, Sid, and June, but only of the other bird he thought he saw in the mirror. And then what a fight there was! He flew at the mirror, pecking at it and banging his wings against it, until he fell on the dressing table, tired out. A moment later, however, he was up and fighting again.

The children needed no-one to read them any stories now. They had plenty to interest them.

© Studio Lisa

Having a bird house is great fun.

And more was to come. For all of a sudden, to their great surprise, another bird flew into their bedroom and perched on the dressing table beside the first one. At this, the first bird started to fight the bird in the mirror again, even more furiously than before. At last, quite exhausted, it dropped on the table and looked feebly at its mate.

Which one spied the straw first I don't know.

But one of them did. There was only a little of it, and it was on the top shelf in a corner of the bedroom. But first one bird saw it, and then the other, and in less time than it takes to tell they were both up there busily building a nest!

You can guess how happy the children were now, and how pleased they were that they had been so friendly to the birds in the garden, and made them bird houses!

Day after day those two birds flew in and out of the children's bedroom as if it belonged to them. They never seemed to notice them, and certainly they weren't bothered by the fact that they all had measles.

Then one day Roger climbed up to the top shelf and let out a yell.

"Eggs!" he cried. "Four of them. We'll soon have some baby birds hatched in our bedroom!"

And he was right. Before the last of the three children was over the measles, and up and about again, four tiny heads and four wide-open mouths appeared over the edge of the shelf.

Later came the first flying lessons, with the three children in grandstand seats, looking on. And then at last the sad day arrived when the nest was forsaken, and the fun was over.

If you were to meet Roger, Sid, and June to-day, and ask them about the time they had the measles, all they would remember would be about the little feathered friends who came to stay with them and turned their sorrow into joy.

Printed and published in Great Britain by The Stanborough Press Ltd., Watford, Herts.   25M/619/1152